DATE DUE

THE PHILHARMONIC GETS DRESSED

THE PHILHARMONIC GETS DRESSED

by Karla Kuskin

illustrations by Marc Simont

HarperCollins*Publishers*

The Philharmonic Gets Dressed
Text copyright © 1982 by Karla Kuskin
Illustrations copyright © 1982 by Marc Simont
All rights reserved. No part of this book may be used or
reproduced in any manner whatsoever without written
permission except in the case of brief quotations embodied
in critical articles and reviews. Manufactured in China.
For information address HarperCollins
Children's Books, a division of HarperCollins Publishers,
10 East 53rd Street, New York, NY 10022.

Library of Congress Cataloging-in-Publication Data
Kuskin, Karla.
   The Philharmonic gets dressed.
   "A Charlotte Zolotow book"
   "A Harper Trophy book"
   Summary: The 105 members of the Philharmonic
Orchestra get ready for a performance.
   [1. Clothing and dress—Fiction.
2. Orchestra—Fiction] I. Simont, Marc, ill.
II. Title.
PZ7.K965Ph   [E]   81-48658
ISBN 0-06-023622-1   AACR2
ISBN 0-06-023623-X (lib. bdg.)
ISBN 0-06-443124-X (pbk.)

This began with Charlie's "tail."

It is almost Friday night. Outside, the dark is getting darker
and the cold is getting colder. In-
side, lights are coming on in houses

and apartment buildings. And here and there, uptown and downtown and across the bridges of the city, one hundred and five people are getting dressed to go to work.

First they get washed. There are ninety-two men and thirteen women. Many take showers. A few take baths. Two men and three women run bubblebaths, and one man reads in the tub while the cat watches. One woman sits in the bubbles and sings.

When they have finished washing, they dry. They use big towels and little towels and a lot of dusting powder. All the men shave except for three, who have beards. Two trim.

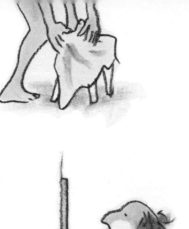

Then, when the one hundred
and five people are showered and
bathed, shaved and toweled, dusted
and dry, they put on their underwear.

The men wear undershorts or briefs. Some of the men wear T-shirt undershirts with sleeves. Some wear undershirts without sleeves, and a

few of the ninety-two do not wear undershirts at all. But night and the temperature are falling, and one thin man buttons up a suit of long-sleeved, long-legged underwear.

All the men put on black socks. There are short socks and long socks and fancy silk socks that have decorations called clocks. Some of the men wear leg garters to keep the long socks from falling down around their ankles.

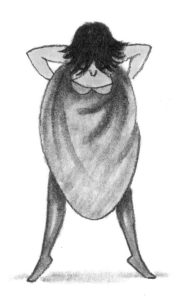

The thirteen women put on different kinds of complicated underwear: underpants, panty hose or stockings, petticoats or slips, and brassieres. One woman whose feet always freeze pulls on wool socks over her stockings.

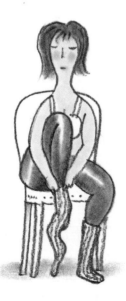

When all the men have their underwear on, they get into long-sleeved white shirts and button them up. Then they put on black trousers. Forty-five men stand up to

get into their pants. Forty-seven sit
down. Each pair of pants has a shiny
black stripe down the outside of
each leg. The men zip zippers and
button a button or two.

One man has wavy black hair
streaked with white, like lightning.
He puts on a very soft white shirt

with ruffles down the front. It has special cuffs that fasten with cuff links. This man hooks a wide black cloth belt around his waist. The belt is called a cummerbund. None of the other men wear belts with their pants. They button suspenders onto the waistlines of their pants and snap the suspenders over their shoulders.

Eight women dress in long black skirts. They wear black tops, sweaters, or blouses. Four women put on long black dresses. And one wears a black jumper over a black shirt. A

few of the women put jewelry on, a
necklace, earrings, but no bracelets.
Bracelets would get in the way when
they're working.

All the men put on black bow ties. Some tie them on in front of mirrors. Some stare into space and tie them. The thin man whistles a tune as he ties his tie on. Twenty-seven men clip on ties that are already made into bows. The man with the wavy black and white hair, the ruffly shirt, and the cummerbund ties on a *very* big white bow tie. It looks like a white bat. No one

else has a tie like his. He slips on a white vest and then a black jacket that is short in the front and long in the back, where it divides in two, like black beetle wings. The jacket and pants are called tails. Tonight all the other ninety-one men put on tuxedo jackets. These are black too, with shiny satin lapels. But they do not have that beetle wing back.

When all the men and women are completely dressed in black and white, they get ready to go out. They put on overcoats, jackets, or capes, boots or rubbers, mittens or gloves, some scarves, many hats, a few earmuffs. Then almost everyone

picks up a case. The cases are different shapes and shades of black and brown. The man with the dark wavy hair with the white lightning in it, the ruffly shirt, cummerbund, and bow tie that looks like a white bat picks up a very thin leather briefcase. No one else has a case like his.

All the one hundred and five men and women say good-by. Good-by to mothers, fathers, husbands, wives, or friends, children, dogs, birds, a cat— whoever is staying at home.

Then they walk out of one
hundred and five doors, into one
hundred and five streets, and there
they take cabs, cars, subways, or
buses to the middle of the city.

The man with the black and
white wavy hair wears a black coat
with a velvet collar and a white silk
scarf. He steps into a very long car
that is waiting for him outside his

apartment building. While the driver drives, the man opens his case and looks at some papers. He sings a little and hums.

At 8:25 on Friday night in the middle of the city, one hundred and four people walk onto the big stage in Philharmonic Hall. They have left their overcoats, jackets, or capes, boots or rubbers, mittens or gloves, some scarves, many hats, a few earmuffs backstage in dark green

metal lockers. They have left their cases, in different shapes and shades of black and brown, back there too. Now one hundred and one of the men and women are carrying the musical instruments that were in those cases.

Three people do not carry instruments. They are the harpist who
plays the harp, and the two tympan-
ists, who play the kettledrums and
smaller percussion instruments: the
cymbals, a gong. These instruments
are too heavy to carry around. They
are already on the stage.

There are one hundred and two chairs on the stage, and two stools. Near each of these there is a music stand with sheets of music on it. The one hundred and four people take

their seats. The double bass players sit on stools. Everyone turns to the first page of music. It is a white page covered with black lines and musical notes.

The man with the black wavy hair lit with white enters. He walks to the front of the stage and steps one step up onto a box called a podium. There he can be seen very clearly by the one hundred and four

people on the stage and by the
hundreds of people in the audience.
The audience applauds. The man
bows. He is the conductor, the leader
of the orchestra, and he holds a stick
in his hand. It is called a baton,
which is French for stick.

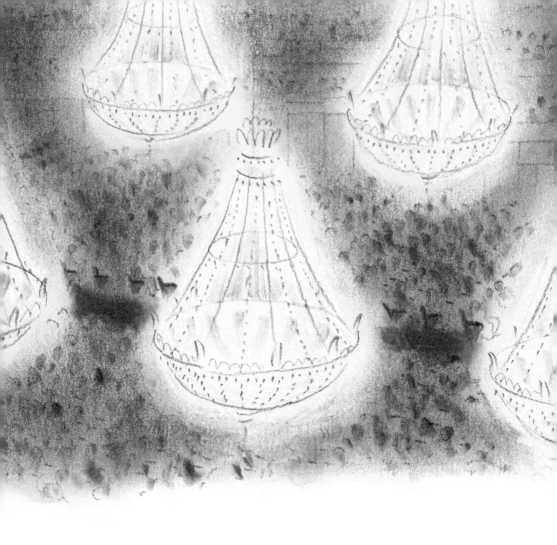

The conductor raises the baton
in the air. Way up, on the ceil-
ing of Philharmonic Hall, six
chandeliers sparkle silently. The

conductor brings the baton down,
and the hall, which is as wide and
long as a red velvet football field,
fills with music.

The music floats and rises. It sings and dances from violas, violins, cellos, double basses, flutes, a piccolo, bassoons, clarinets, oboes, French horns, trumpets, trombones, a tuba, a harp, drums, cymbals, chimes, and one thin silver triangle.

It is 8:30 on Friday night, and the one hundred and five men and women dressed completely in black and white have gone to work turning the black notes on white pages into a symphony.

They are the members of the Philharmonic Orchestra, and their work is to play. Beautifully.